LEVEL

DAYS OF FUTURE PAST

By **Thomas Macri**

Illustrated by **Patrick Olliffe** *and* **Pete Pantazis**

Based on the Marvel comic book series **X-Men**

New York
Los Angeles

marvelkids.com

© 2014 MARVEL

All rights reserved. Published by Marvel Press, an imprint of Disney Book Group. No part of this book may be reproduced or transmitted in any form or by any means, electronic or mechanical, including photocopying, recording, or by any information storage and retrieval system, without written permission from the publisher. For information address Marvel Press, 125 West End Avenue, New York, NY 10023.

Printed in the United States of America

First Edition

1 3 5 7 9 10 8 6 4 2

G658-7729-4-14060

ISBN 978-1-4231-7213-0

SUSTAINABLE FORESTRY INITIATIVE

Certified Chain of Custody
Promoting Sustainable Forestry

www.sfiprogram.org
SFI-01415

The SFI label applies to the text stock

Chapter One: Life in Tomorrow

Twenty years from now, the landscape of New York will look like a war zone.

Giant robots rule the city and all of North America. These machines, called Sentinels, were created to destroy mutants. Some of the hardest mutants to destroy are heroes called the X-Men.

But one by one, even the X-Men fall to the Sentinels. Cyclops, Jean Grey, even the X-Men's leader, Professor X, are defeated.

Two of the last remaining X-Men plan to meet here in what once was Times Square. Because it's so desolate, it's one of the only zones that is not patrolled by the Sentinels. These X-Men have a plan to change their world.

But just because the Sentinels don't patrol the area doesn't mean it's safe!

Kate is attacked by a band of thugs. She was born with the ability to walk through walls and become as light as air. She would use her powers if she could. But the Sentinels have placed a collar around her neck. It prevents her from using her abilities.

Luckily for Kate, her fellow X-Man
Wolverine is still alive. And he is here
to help!

Wolverine is wearing a collar, too.
But he has trained as a samurai. He can
fight well without his powerful claws.

Kate tells Wolverine she's glad to see him. Wolverine has brought something for Kate and the rest of the surviving X-Men. It will neutralize their collars. Their powers will work again!

Many years from the time we live in, the X-Men's world might be a very dark place. But it hasn't always been this way.

Chapter Two: Back to the Past

Twenty years before the Sentinels took over, the X-Men's world was a very different place.

That time is our present day. The
X-Men had discovered a teenage mutant
in the suburbs of Chicago. That mutant's
name was Kate Pryde. She called herself
Kitty then.

For weeks, Kitty Pryde had been
feeling really sick. Her headaches were
terrible. And right before they'd go
away, something very strange would
happen. The day the X-Men arrived at
her home was no different.

Kitty phased right through her bedroom floor and fell into the living room just as the X-Men were arriving. The X-Men's leader, Professor X, was there. So were Wolverine; Storm, who could control the weather; Cyclops, who could shoot force beams from his eyes; and Jean Grey, who could move things with her mind. Kitty's parents didn't know about her powers, so the X-Men took her out to a diner to talk about them.

Storm told Kitty that she was a mutant—a person born with fantastic abilities. Professor X wanted Kitty to come train with the X-Men. This would help her learn to use her powers. Kitty was nervous. But she was more frightened of dealing with her powers on her own. So she agreed to join the X-Men.

Kitty's parents thought that Professor X's school was a regular boarding school. They didn't know that it was a school for mutants. So they let Kitty go with the professor and join his school. Her life would never be the same.

Chapter Three:
Welcome to the X-Men, Kitty Pryde!

The professor gave Kitty a costume.
She felt like a real Super Hero! She'd be
a full-fledged X-Man someday!

And soon it was time for Kitty's first training session. It was set up in the X-Men's special gym—the Danger Room—which could do just about anything! Her goal was simply to cross the room.

As nervous as Kitty was, it proved easy for her to pass the test. She walked with no problem from one end of the room to the other.

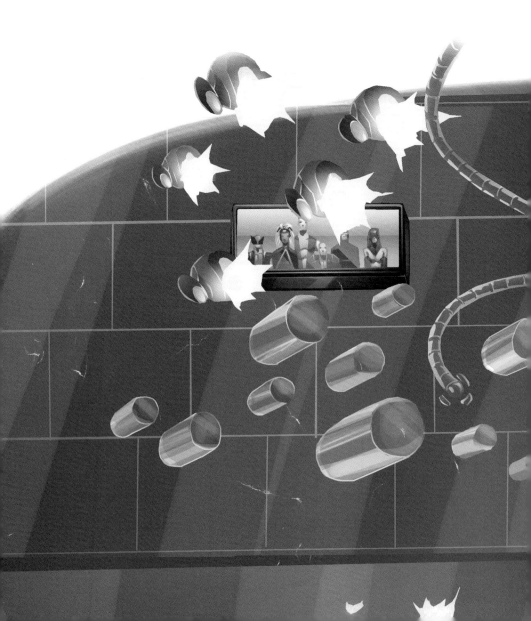

In the control room, the other X-Men laughed. It had taken weeks for the professor to program the Danger Room for the test. And Kitty beat it in less than a minute!

But just as Kitty made it to the door,
she suddenly fainted!

The X-Men rushed over to her.

They couldn't figure out what had happened. Could it have been an enemy attack? They would soon find out that it was exactly the opposite.

Chapter Four: Back to the Future

Back in the future world, the X-Men's plan worked!

Once Wolverine and Kate met up with the rest of the remaining X-Men, they used the device to get their powers back. Rachel Summers, the future daughter of Cyclops and Jean Grey, used her amazing psionic powers on Kate. She can read minds and even move things just by thought! Rachel sent Kate's mind back into her teenage body.

The X-Men know a series of key
events had brought on the state of their
world. Those events began with the
Brotherhood of Mutants kidnapping

presidential candidate Senator Robert Kelly.

The X-Men think that sending Kate
back to stop the kidnapping will prevent
this future.

But while Kate was in our era, Kitty is in the future X-Men's time. They need to do everything they can to protect her. If Kate's body is hurt, Kitty might not ever be able to return.

With their powers back, the heroes are able to fight the Sentinels. But countless robots attack the X-Men, and they are not sure how long they can hold out. Back in the past, Kate would need to hurry!

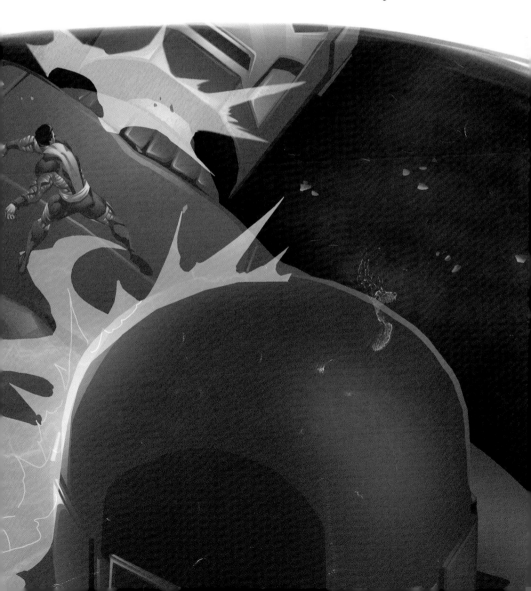

Chapter Five:
The Brotherhood Strikes

"Cyclops! Jean! You're alive!" Kitty shouted.

The X-Men had no idea what was going on. Of course they were alive. Kitty explained that she had traveled from the future. The only way to stop

their horrible future from coming
to pass was to prevent the senator's
kidnapping.

Jean Grey had the power to read
minds. "I've scanned her mind and she's
telling the truth!" Jean said.

"Then there's no time to lose!"
Cyclops said.

And the X-Men rushed to the Senate
chamber in Washington, D.C.

When the X-Men arrived, the
Brotherhood had already broken into
the chamber. But they hadn't yet
kidnapped the senator. The Brotherhood
thought mutants were better than

humans and were meant to rule them.

The X-Men thought humans and mutants should live together peacefully. And that might never happen if they didn't stop the Brotherhood.

Chapter Six: Saving Kate

Meanwhile, the future hadn't yet changed at all. The Sentinels chase after the X-Men. And the robots are not giving up.

"I'll hold off these Sentinels," Storm calls out. "Keep Kate safe at all costs!"

"I'll give Storm a hand!" Wolverine shouts as he attacks a pair of Sentinels. "Colossus, we could use some help!"

"Rachel, it's up to you to protect Kate.
I have faith in you!" Colossus says.

"If I fail . . ." Rachel responds.

"You will not, you *cannot,* fail! The
world depends on you!" Colossus tells her.

Colossus joins his fellow X-Men in
their fight.

And Rachel does all she can to protect
Kate Pryde.

Chapter Seven: Time's Up!

Meanwhile, in our time, the Brotherhood's leader, Mystique, told Senator Kelly to come with her.

"If you want the senator, you're going to have to go through us!" Wolverine said.

"That will be my pleasure," Mystique replied.

The Brotherhood of Mutants attacked.
And the X-Men attacked right back.

The mutant called Pyro blasted
Colossus with fire. But Colossus's metal
body didn't burn.

"Look out behind you!" the mutant known as Destiny cried out to Avalanche, another member of the Brotherhood.

Destiny could see the future, and she knew Storm was about to attack. Avalanche started to crumble walls around Storm, but Jean Grey was able to stop the bricks from falling. This left Storm able to capture both Avalanche and Destiny in a whirlwind.

The Blob, another member of the Brotherhood, couldn't be moved.

The X-Men tried as best they could, but it was no use.

"We might not be able to move you, Blob," Colossus said. "But we can move the ground beneath you!"

And with that, Colossus smashed a huge crater under the Blob's feet, sending him into it. Storm cemented the Blob into the crater with thick sheets of ice.

But in all the commotion, the X-Men had lost track of the Brotherhood's leader, Mystique. Her power was to change her shape. She had disguised herself as a government worker who was trying to protect the senator. Once she had him cornered, she showed her true colors.

"You're coming with me, Senator. Mutants are superior to humans, and we will rule over you."

Mystique pointed a high-tech crossbow at the senator.

"Not today you won't—not ever!" Kitty cried as she phased through Mystique. She was able to prevent Mystique's bow from hitting the senator, and she knocked Mystique out in the process. The other X-Men moved in to capture her!

Just then, Kitty started to faint
again. But this time the X-Men knew
what was happening. Rachel had
succeeded in keeping Kate safe in the
future. And the X-Men had prevented
the kidnapping in our time.

But had they changed the future?
Only time would tell. But one thing was
for sure: the X-Men had saved the day.